Published by Greenleaf Book Group Press
Austin, Texas
www.gbgpress.com

Distributed by Greenleaf Book Group

For ordering information or special discounts for bulk purchases, please contact Greenleaf Book Group at PO Box 91869, Austin, TX 78709, 512.891.6100.

Design and composition by Greenleaf Book Group
Cover design by Greenleaf Book Group
Illustrations by Stephanie Dehennin

Cataloging-in-Publication data is available.

Print ISBN: 978-1-62634-347-4
eBook ISBN: 978-1-62634-348-1

Part of the Tree Neutral® program, which offsets the number of trees consumed in the production and printing of this book by taking proactive steps, such as planting trees in direct proportion to the number of trees used: www.treeneutral.com

Manufactured through Asia Pacific Offset on acid-free paper
Manufactured in Guang Dong, China on June, 2019
Batch No. Q19050034

19 20 21 21 22 23 24 25   13 12 11 10 9 8 7 6

First Edition

The First Book in The Live Big Series

DREAM BIG

A Mythological Fable About Animals
Who Discover How to Live Their Best Lives

KAT KRONENBERG

illustrated by Stephanie Dehennin

GREENLEAF
BOOK GROUP PRESS

Contained within these books is a powerful scientific fact that stars live **above us**, around us, and within us all. Watch the animals uncover a secret to lighting the stars within their hearts. Try their secret and celebrate your best life too!

Long ago in the wilds of East Africa, when the savannas were new, this moody Baboon discovered a powerful secret— SHHH—

It began one starry night when
Caterpillar looked up at a twinkling star
and whispered, "Oh, I wish I could be
like Bird and fly."

Baboon heard and couldn't help but sneer,
"Wa-Hu-Wa-Hu-Wa-How can you fly with all
those feet clinging onto that tree?"

"Oh no! You're right," Caterpillar
cried and spun a cocoon to hide.

But Caterpillar still kept dreaming.

Finally Caterpillar broke free. Looking up at his star,

he smiled big in who he is and clapped, "But I can! I believe."

Yes! Caterpillar grew wings!

And Baboon's eyes popped out of his head as that first butterfly flew by and said,

"Look at me! A bug who started with 16 feet can fly like a bird because I believed in myself and my dream."*

* Caterpillars transform and emerge from their cocoons with wings, becoming Butterflys.

Excited, the next starry night Baboon
started playing his drum when
he noticed Tadpole wish upon his
twinkling star, "Oh, I wish I could
dance and sing to that cool drum beat."

Baboon puffed out his chest with pride, but
still he sneered,
  "Wa-Hu-Wa-Hu-Wa-How can you dance?
You got NO FEET to follow A BEAT."

"Oh no! You're right," Tadpole cried and swam
so deep in despair that his tail started to shrink.

But Tadpole still longed to dance.

Finally Tadpole turned and swam back to the surface.

Looking up at his star, he smiled big in who he is
and clapped, "But I can! I believe."

WHOOSH! WHAM! YOU CAN DO ANYTHING!

Yes! Tadpole grew feet! And Baboon fell to his knees from all he'd just seen, but kept pounding his drum to be in the fun as that first Frog hopped to the beat singing, "Ribbit! Ribbit! Dream it! Live it!"*

* Tadpoles absorb their tails, grow four legs, and lungs to dance and sing on land as Frogs.

The next starry night Baboon, who wanted his dream too, got close when he saw Flamingo wish upon her twinkling star, "Oh, how I wish for beauty."

But moody Baboon
still had to sneer,
"Wa-Hu-Wa-Hu-Wa-Why
beauty? You're too ordinary?"

21

"Oh no! You're right," Flamingo cried in
such pain that she turned an awful gray.

But Flamingo still hoped for beauty.

Finally Flamingo felt her beauty within.

Looking up at her star, she smiled big in who she is
and clapped, "But I can! I believe."

WHOOSH! WHAM! YOU CAN HAVE ANYTHING!

Yes! Flamingo turned an amazing shade of pink! And this time Baboon tried to catch her wished-upon star, but he missed and fell down hard.

Now he lay back in pain, scratching his head as Flamingo flew by and said, "Look at me! I'm extraordinary! Please, never give up on your dreams. We're all full of possibility—even you, moody Baboon."*

* Flamingos are born white, turning an awful shade of grey before turning a beautiful pink color.

The next starry night, Baboon thinks he figured out their— SHHH—Secret. So he finds his twinkling star and makes a wish, "Oh, I really wish to celebrate everyone's dream coming true and encourage others, too!"

But then Baboon sneered at himself,
"Wa-Who-Wa-Who-Wa-Who would even
come to my celebration? I've been a buffoon
of a baboon!"

Alone and miserable, Termite stood near
and sneered, "No one."

29

"Oh no! You're right," Baboon cried as he
covered his face in shame.

But Baboon still kept imagining ways to celebrate.

Finally Baboon uncovered his face.

Looking up at his star, he smiled big in who he is
and boom-clapped, "But I can! I believe."

WHOOSH! WHAM! YOU CAN CELEBRATE YOUR LIFE!

Yes! Baboon radiated fun, and everyone actually came as he passed out pompoms and drums for his Boom Shake Celebration:

"Wa~Whoo~
Shake your pompoms.
Shake and know
You guys are Heroes!
To show us how—"*

* Baboons can be very moody, bossy, and mean. They can also be very happy, helpful, and playful.

34

But Baboon stopped mid-cheer because someone wasn't there. Who was missing?

Termite! Baboon had seen her wish upon a star for
a home like the bees, filled with friends and family.

Instead Termite dug a hole, and Baboon found her all alone.
She'd been too afraid to try.

So Baboon got Frog,

and together they wrote her a song:

Twinkle, twinkle, little star
Smile BIG in who you are
Clap "I can" and dare believe
Dreams come true for you and me
We will wish upon our star
Guiding us we will go far!*

* Baby Baboon and Frog's song is sung to the tune of "Twinkle, Twinkle, Little Star." Sing along!

After the song, Termite, looking up at her star,
smiled big in who she is and clapped, "But I can! I believe."

WHOOSH! WHAM! YOU CAN LOVE AND BE LOVED!

Yes! Termite built a giant castle full of love, fun, friends and family!

They even crowned Termite queen as she bowed and said, "If someone as miserable as me can live her dream, you can too. So please, try the secret—SHHH! Wish upon your star, SMILE big in who you are and BELIEVE!"*

* Termites work together to build amazing castles filled with a Queen, soldiers, workers, and so much more.

43

With that, Baboon and his new found friends
finished his Boom Shake Celebration:

"Wa-Whoo!
Shake your pompoms.
Drum. Dream. Smile.
Light your stardust,
You will go miles!"

NOTES FOR TWO-LEGGERS OF ALL AGES:

—SHHH—

Study these fascinating animals on Kat's website. We can learn so much from their lives. Plus, The Secret they use is so powerful that Baby Baboon wants to make sure we understand these important keys to their discovery—

* ★ Stars are scientifically proven to live within us, around us, and above us. At night, the stars above twinkle with our dreams, reminding us that—

* ★ We have hearts of stars: stars hidden in our chest just waiting to be lit.

* ★ To light this priceless, timeless treasure hidden in our chests, we must SMILE & BELIEVE. The African Animals call it catching CATCH-M:

CATCH-M is the name of the marvelous, miraculous wished-upon star, who can *WHOOSH* into our lives when invited by our smiles to **WHAM!** ignite through our belief the gift of stars in our hearts, giving us the extra faith and courage we need to achieve our DREAMS.

Baby Baboon came up with this catchy nickname as our reminder. She also has some fun things you can do alone, with family, friends, or in a classroom before you go on your own adventure to "catch CATCH-M" too!

(Share your fun with our LIVE BIG COMMUNITY using a #LiveBIG #CatchM on social media.)

1. Build a Dream Board

"Everyone has inside them a piece of good news. The good news is you don't know how great you can be! How much you can love! What you can accomplish! And what your potential is."—Anne Frank

Get to know your dream by creating visuals that help you better define your goals. Cut out sayings from magazines or newspapers that inspire you, photos of heroes who encourage you, and draw, create whatever else you think can motivate you.

Build a collage from all these on your own, with family, friends, or your class. Then place your Dream Board somewhere you can see it everyday as an encouragement and a reminder that life is a grander adventure when you wake up with a dream to achieve, goals to pursue, and something purposeful to do.

"All our dreams can come true, if we have the courage to pursue them."—Walt Disney

2. Make a "You Can" Drum

Be like Baboon! Make a drum with whatever materials you have to keep your "moody" moods in check & stay motivated to go after your dreams too.

Fill the drum with your dreams—add ideas on how to make them come true, heroes to inspire you, quotes to encourage you, or use the "You Can Cans" download on Kat's website.

Seal the drum. Play away. Even make a "DRUM CIRCLE" with friends, family, your class, even your four-legged friends, and imagine your dream as you dance and sing to a Boom Shake Celebration Song.

> "The drum circle offers equality because there is no head or tail. It includes people of all ages. The main objective is to share rhythm and get in tune with each other and themselves. To form a group consciousness. To entrain and resonate. By entrainment, I mean that a new voice, a collective voice, merges from the group as they drum together."—Mickey Hart of the Grateful Dead

Also, have a blast drumming together as you learn how to play the "**A-BUN-DANCE GAME**" from Kat's website. When the game ends, shout out together, "Our lives are full of abundance!"

3. Make a PomPom/Dream Catcher

> "I want to take all the pain that I feel and celebrate and turn it around."—Stevie Wonder

Be like Baby Baboon! Create a Dream Device that you can use as a PomPom or Dream Catcher to keep your "moody" moods in check and stay encouraged too:

A. Make a hoop with a handle using any material you have—hangers, wire, duct tape, vines, old bracelets, sticks . . . the list is endless.

B. Create "fluff" by attaching any item you can find to the hoop or handle—strips of paper, leaves, feathers, yarn, pieces of fabric, etc.

C. At night, use the handle to hang your Dream Device over your bed like a Dream Catcher. The fluff will catch any bad dreams, and the good dreams will be allowed to pass through to you.

D. During the day, whenever you feel moody or blue, shake the handle of your Dream Device like a PomPom to CELEBRATE your life and remember the power of a smile to help make your dream come true!

> "The more you praise and celebrate your life, the more there is in life to celebrate."—Oprah Winfrey

4. Create CATCH-M, Notes, and Termite Tricks

Student says, "I am very discouraged! What should I do?" Master says, "Encourage others!" —Zen Proverb

Stay motivated for your dreams by finding ways to encourage others to dream big too!
Here are a few ideas:

A. Create your **CATCH-M**: Draw a smile that comes all the way up from your belly, through your chest, and shines from your face who you are. Your wished-upon star continually reflects back this smile's light and love to remind you to keep believing in yourself and your dream.
    Then take your drawn smiles on **CATCH-M ADVENTURES** together: on a field trip, to dinner, or anywhere. On your journey, remind and encourage others to dream big and celebrate their smiles too. Even take pictures and journal as you do.

B. Share "Surprise Smiles," a download on Kat's website. Send notes to friends, family, classmates, or even passersby, that encourage them to SMILE big and believe! Or download the "LOVE BIG GRAM," a free APP on the homepage of Kat's website.

C. In *Dream Big*, Termite and her friends came up with TERMITE TRICKS to encourage others to chase their dreams—did you notice? Go back through the book and see if you can figure them out. Then, use them as inspiration to create your own!

    - Page 43: What message did Termite's friends write on her giant castle as the animals celebrated her dream coming true?

    - Page 44: Termite and her friends wrote the letters "U", "K", and "N" on their backs as an inspirational message to us. Can you decode the meaning?

D. Here's a riddle passed down by Termite and her friends for generations . . . it also happens to be my very favorite! See if you can solve it.

    A _ _ _ _ _ is contagious.

    A _ _ _ _ _ can increase your face value.

    A _ _ _ _ _ can change your mood, the energy in a room, the events of a day—making better all along the way.

    A _ _ _ _ _ can go anywhere. Speak any language. Tug on any heart.

    A _ _ _ _ _ invites the divine light of CATCH-M into your life.

    Now fill in the blank. A _ _ _ _ _! Never forget its power!

(Answers: P. 43—Be You and Smile; P. 44—You Can; SMILE—fills in the blank to my favorite riddle above.)

To celebrate your dreams, find more fun and games, see some "You Can" Drums, PomPoms, and people's CATCH-M's, go to Kat's website: www.katkronenberg.com

Now it is your turn: GO! ENJOY A STARRY NIGHT, and try The—SHHH—Secret too!

There is no telling what you can do . . .

Lay your head back.

Close your eyes.

Take three deep breaths.

Imagine your dream.

Pick your star.

SMILE big in who you are.

Clap "I CAN! I BELIEVE!"

And—Whoosh! Wham!

You can . . .

(The proceeds from *Dream Big* will go to support other Two-Legger's dreams at www.we.org, www.grameen.org, and www.donorschoose.org.)

"A smile is a 'U-SHAPED BRIDGE' that can connect us to everything—our head to our hearts, our lives to one another, and our dreams to the power of something GREATER! So go catch CATCH-M too, and celebrate the great things you can do!" —Kat Kronenberg